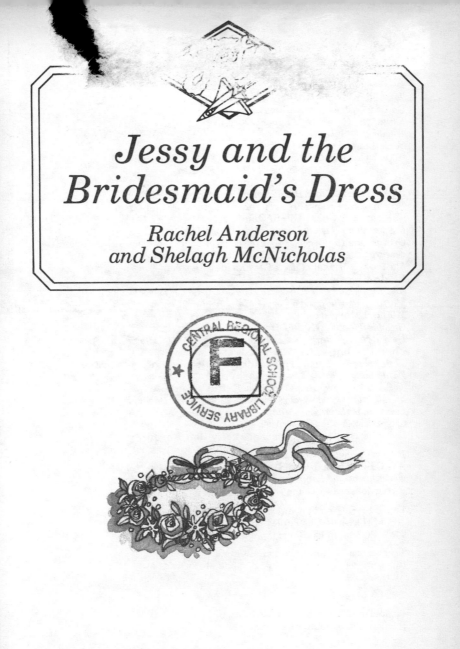

Jessy and the Bridesmaid's Dress

Rachel Anderson
and Shelagh McNicholas

Young Lions

First published in Great Britain by
A & C Black (Publishers) Ltd in 1993
as *Jessy and the Long-Short Dress*
First published in Young Lions 1994

Young Lions is an imprint of the Children's Division
part of HarperCollins Publishers Ltd.
77/85 Fulham Palace Road, London W6 8JB

ISBN 0–00–647493–1

Printed and bound in Great Britain by
HarperCollins Manufacturing, Glasgow

On Saturday mornings, Jessy liked going down the High Street with her mum.

It was nice doing something special, just her and her mum together, while Anna stayed at home and did something special with their dad.

She liked walking slowly past the shops

and looking at all the things in the windows.

The best shop was just before they got to the Post Office. It was a dress shop.

Sometimes Mum was in a hurry and
then there wasn't time to stop.

5

But on other days, Jessy's mum said she had all the time in the world. Then Jessy could stand outside the dress shop looking at the lovely white dress for as long as she wanted.

That's a wedding dress. People often wear a specially beautiful dress like that when they get married.

Ah! Married!

Jessy's family had to explain
things quite carefully to her because
she wasn't very quick at learning.

Then, one day when Jessy and her mum stopped to look in the window of the bridal shop, the dress wasn't there any more. There was just a dull brown suit on display.

I expect someone's bought it.

Gone!

And in the afternoon when Jessy, Anna, and Mum were taking Waffle for his walk to the park, they passed a crowd of people on the pavement outside the church. They were waiting for something.

Ooh look Mum! It's a wedding.

Anna squeezed through the crowd to get a better view.

Jessy saw the bride was wearing the lovely dress. She had flowers in her hair, too.

Jessy decided she wanted to get married and wear a lovely dress and have flowers in her hair.

Anna said, 'First you have to have someone you love.'

Marry Anna?

No, you can't marry me. I'm your sister.

Even though Anna was younger than Jessy, Anna sometimes had to explain things to her sister.

When they got home, Mum found some old bits and pieces to dress up in, and Jessy and Anna played a game of weddings until it was time for tea.

It was fun dressing up.
But what Jessy
really wanted was
to wear a proper
wedding dress.

'Actually,' said Anna, 'I probably
won't ever get married.
Not everybody does. Think of
Aunty Pat. She didn't.'

'And anyway, I think pretty dresses are a nuisance. I like wearing shorts best and then you can

jump

and run

and climb trees and have more proper fun.'

But Jessy didn't want to jump or
run and she wasn't any good at
climbing trees. So they played with
Waffle until Waffle got silly and
over-excited.

On Monday, Jessy came home from school feeling so sad that she didn't even want her tea.

What's up?

What's the matter Jessy?

Teacher going. My Miss Wright.

Jessy went to a special school for children with learning difficulties and she was very fond of her teacher.

In her schoolbag, Jessy had a letter from her school which explained that Miss Wright would be leaving at the end of term.

Orchard House
Special School
Orchard Place.

Tel: 27243

8 April 1993

Dear Parents,

Miss Wright, who takes our class 3, has been on our staff for three and a half years. Sadly she will be leaving at the end of the Summer term, to take up an appointment in another part of the country.

There will be a party in the school hall on Wednesday 21st to say goodbye and past pupils are most welcome.

Yours sincerely
R. Thomas

R. Thomas
Head Teacher.

'What a pity,' said Mum.
'She's so nice.'

The very next day after school,
Miss Wright herself came round
to Jessy's home.

Anna was surprised, for teachers
don't often come to people's homes.
Miss Wright had some interesting
news. As well as moving, she was
going to be married.

And she wanted Jessy to be a bridesmaid.

'You see,' she said, 'Jessy and I both started at Orchard Place on the same day, so she's always been rather special to me.'

'Bridesmaid?' said Jessy.
'You remember,' said Anna, 'That's the person who walks behind the bride, helping with her dress and holding the flowers.'

Yes! Be a bridesmaid.

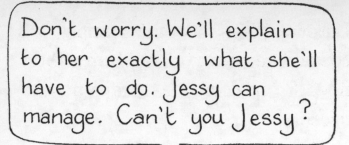

Don't worry. We'll explain to her exactly what she'll have to do. Jessy can manage. Can't you Jessy?

Jessy wasn't sure. Mostly, when she got in a muddle, her sister was there to help her.

Anna too?

'No Jessy,' said Mum, 'Miss Wright hasn't asked Anna. She's asked you. You're her special person.'

Later on, Miss Wright brought
round the things that Mum would
need for making the bridesmaid's
dress,

a paper pattern

five metres of blue
silky fabric

a roll of blue thread

a blue zip fastener

two metres of
lace edging

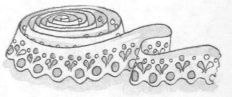

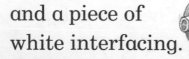

some blue ribbon

and a piece of
white interfacing.

Mum got out the sewing-machine,

and the very
sharp scissors

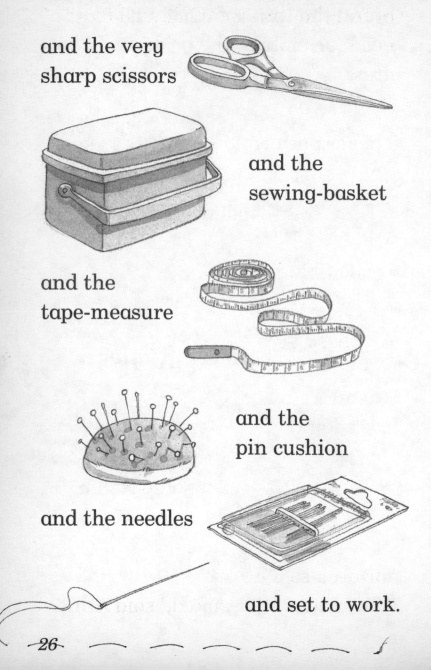

and the
sewing-basket

and the
tape-measure

and the
pin cushion

and the needles

and set to work.

'Oho!' said Jessy's dad when he got in from his work. 'What's all this?'

'Brides,' said Jessy.
'She means bridesmaid,' said Anna.

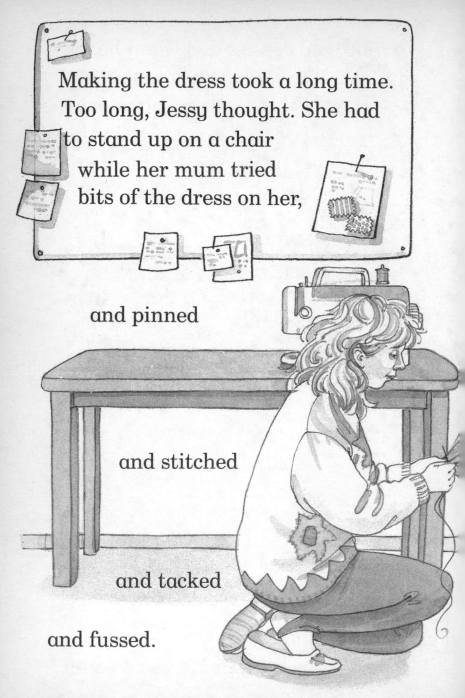

Making the dress took a long time. Too long, Jessy thought. She had to stand up on a chair while her mum tried bits of the dress on her,

and pinned

and stitched

and tacked

and fussed.

Jessy could hear Anna having a good time in the garden playing football with Dad.

Keep still Jessy there's a good girl. Otherwise I can't get it right, and you don't want to look a fright do you now?

Usually, Waffle liked joining in with ball-games but now he preferred to watch the dress-making.

30

Anna said, 'Waffle seems very interested in your dress, doesn't he?'

Perhaps he wants to be a bridesmaid too?

'I think we'd better keep the door
closed when we're not in here,'
said Mum when she stopped sewing
for the day. 'We don't want
Waffle going in there on his own.
You never know what he might
get up to!'

Anna wrote a notice to make sure
nobody forgot about the door.

At last the dress was finished.

It was a long dress
with a wide sash,
big floppy ruffled
sleeves, and a lacy collar.
It was the most lovely dress
that Jessy had ever seen,
even better than the bride's
one that used to be in the
shop window.

Jessy was pleased that her mum
had made it so well.

There was a white petticoat
to go with the dress,

and a wreath
of flowers
for Jessy's head,

and new
shoes and socks.

'Oh Jessy, what a nice dress,' said Anna. 'You look really good. Do us a twirl to make the skirt go out.'

The evening before the wedding, there was a practice at the church where Miss Wright was to be married.

Wear my new dress?

No, it's just a practice now so you wear ordinary clothes.

There was a lot to remember so Jessy had to listen carefully.

She had to look after the very small niece, whose name was Rosie.

They had to walk together side by
side, not too fast and not too slow,
keeping just behind Miss Wright
and trying not to
step on her
heels.

Jessy also had to remember where they were meant to stop walking,

when they were meant to start singing,

when they were meant to keep quite quiet,

and when Miss Wright would turn round and give Jessy the bouquet of flowers.

Jessy would have to hold these flowers carefully until it was time to hand them back.

And all the time, Jessy and Rosie were supposed to keep quiet and not be silly.

When Mum and Jessy got home,
Mum said,

Anna was coming to the wedding
too, but she would be wearing her
ordinary best clothes and sitting
with Mum and Dad and all the
other guests.

Jessy was so excited
about tomorrow
that she went to
have
one last,
quick,
teeny,
tiny peep . . .

Close
the
door!

. . . at the bridesmaid's dress.

She was so excited that she didn't notice Waffle waiting just outside

the door as she hurried upstairs,

and joined Anna in the bath.

43

When Anna and Jessy came downstairs to have their hair dried . . .

. . . they met Waffle sitting on the stairs. He was looking pleased with himself.

He was wearing something blue and
silky on his head which looked like
an old-fashioned lady's bonnet.
He looked very funny.

Wruff!!

'I think it's a dog's hat!' said Anna.

At first everybody laughed. But
then they saw that it wasn't a
smart hat after all.

On his head, Waffle was wearing
half a blue silky sleeve which had
been ripped from a bridesmaid's
dress by a pair of very sharp teeth.

Oh no!

Everybody stared and stared at the mess of the dress. Waffle had had a wonderful time with it.

And with the new shoes.
And with the new socks.

'It's ruined,' said Anna.
'Oh my, this is a mess-up,' said Dad.
Jessy thought she was probably
going to cry.

Waffle wagged his tail hopefully.
But when nobody told him what a
good boy he was, he put his head on
one side and his smart dog's hat
slipped off. Mum picked it up.

Stupid dog!

'Naughty Waffle. Bad dog,'
said Jessy.
'You could borrow my best dress.'
said Anna.
Jessy shook her head. 'No good,'
she said.

'And the shoes would be
okay if I had a go
at them with some
blue polish,' said Dad.

'And look, the
wreath is quite all
right,' said Anna.
'He hasn't even
touched it.'

Jessy shook her head.

Can't go.
No long dress.

Of course you can still go. It's not what a person looks like that matters. It's what they do and how they do it.

But she can't wear the dress all chewed like that!

The most important thing is that Miss Wright is going to marry the person she loves. But still, I'll see what I can do.

And she set to work at once.

All evening, she snipped, and clipped, and tucked and tacked, and folded and pinned and patched.

Waffle stayed outside in the garden looking sad.

Jessy knew that it wasn't Waffle's fault. He was only a dog. He didn't understand what he'd done.

Mum didn't even stop for supper.

When Jessy and Anna went up to
bed, Mum was still at work. By
morning Mum had re-made what
was left of the dress into a new one.

It wasn't quite the same as before. The sleeves weren't as big and floppy and the skirt was a lot shorter. But it was still a very nice dress and Jessy knew that her mum was the best mum in the world to try so hard for her.

'Ooh, Jessy you're so beautiful now! Like an angel with a halo of flowers,' said Anna, as Mum finished fixing the wreath round Jessy's head. Anna gave her sister a hug.

Jessy went to the loo one last time,

Better safe than sorry!

and so did Anna. Then they set off
for the wedding.

At the church, there were crowds of people and everybody was ready and waiting for Miss Wright. Rosie was wearing a dress which looked just like Jessy's had before Waffle got at it. She pointed at Jessy.

Her dress is silly. Not like mine.

Anna said, 'Jessy's older than you. So she has a special long-short dress.'

When Miss Wright arrived, she smiled but she didn't say anything about anybody's dress. And inside the church, everything went just right.

Jessy remembered to do exactly as she'd been asked, and joined in with all the cheerful singing. Rosie mostly behaved quite properly and only lay down on the floor once.

At the party afterwards,

the bride (who used to be Jessy's
teacher and was now a married
person) gave Jessy a kiss.

And her new husband told
everybody in the room what
excellent bridesmaids Jessy and
Rosie had been.

Then the grownups talked and danced while Jessy and Rosie and Anna ate cake. And Jessy knew that this was one of the happiest days of her life.